Sophie Jewett

The Pilgrim and Other Poems

Sophie Jewett

The Pilgrim and Other Poems

ISBN/EAN: 9783337290061

Printed in Europe, USA, Canada, Australia, Japan

Cover: Foto ©Andreas Hilbeck / pixelio.de

More available books at **www.hansebooks.com**

HE PILGRIM AND OTHER POEMS

THE PILGRIM

AND OTHER POEMS

BY

OPHIE ... T

ELLEN ...

To

H. H. H.

CONTENTS

THE PILGRIM

THE PILGRIM

" Such a palmer ne'er was seene,
 Lesse Love himselfe had palmer beene."
                                          Never too Late.

Pilgrim feet, pray whither bound?
Pilgrim eyes, pray whither bent?
Sandal-shod and travel-gowned,
Lo, I seek the way they went
Late who passed toward Holy Land.

Pilgrim, it was long ago ;
None remains who saw that band ;
Grass and forest overgrow
Every path their footing wore.
Men are wise ; they seek no more
Roads that lead to Holy Land.

Proud his look, as who should say :
I shall find where lies the way.

Pilgrim, thou art fair of face,
Staff and scrip are not for thee ;

Gentle pilgrim, of thy grace,
Leave thy quest, and bide with me.
Love shall serve thee, joy shall bless;
Thou wert made for tenderness:
God's green world is fair and sweet;
Not o'er sea and Eastern strand,
But where friend and lover meet
Lies the way to Holy Land.

Low his voice, his lashes wet:
One day if God will— not yet.

Pilgrim, pardon me and heed.
Men of old who took that way
Went for fame of goodly deed,
Or, if sooth the stories say,
Sandalled priest, or knight in selle,
Flying each in pain and hate,
Harassed by stout fiends of hell,
Sought his crime to expiate.
Prithee, Pilgrim, go not hence;
Clear thy brow, and white thy hand,
What shouldst thou with penitence?
Wherefore seek to Holy Land?

Stern the whisper on his lip :
Sin and shame are in my scrip.

Pilgrim, pass, since it must be ;
Take thy staff, and have thy will ;
Prayer and love shall follow thee ;
I will watch thee o'er the hill.
What thy fortune God doth know ;
By what paths thy feet must go.
Far and dim the distance lies,
Yet my spirit prophesies :
Not in vigil lone and late,
Bowed upon the tropic sand,
But within the city gate,
In the struggle of the street,
Suddenly thine eyes shall meet
His whose look is Holy Land.

Smiled the pilgrim, sad and sage :
Long must be my pilgrimage.

SONNETS

THE SOLDIER

"Non vi si pensa quanto sangue costa."
Paradiso xxix. 91.

THE soldier fought his battle silently.
   Not his the strife that stays for set of sun ;
   It seemed this warfare never might be done ;
   Through glaring day and blinding night fought he.
There came no hand to help, no eye to see ;
   No herald's voice proclaimed the fight begun ;
   No trumpet, when the bitter field was won,
   Sounded abroad the soldier's victory.
As if the struggle had been light, he went,
   Gladly, life's common road a little space ;
   Nor any knew how his heart's blood was spent ;
Yet there were some who after testified
   They saw a glory grow upon his face ;
   And all men praised the soldier when he died.

9

A FRIENDSHIP

SMALL fellowship of daily commonplace
    We hold together, dear, constrained to go
    Diverging ways.   Yet day by day I know
    My life is sweeter for thy life's sweet grace ;
And if we meet but for a moment's space,
    Thy touch, thy word, sets all the world aglow.
    Faith soars serener, haunting doubts shrink low,
    Abashed before the sunshine of thy face.

Nor press of crowd, nor waste of distance serves
    To part us.   Every hush of evening brings
    Some hint of thee, true-hearted friend of mine ;
And as the farther planet thrills and swerves
    When towards it through the darkness Saturn swings,
    Even so my spirit feels the spell of thine.

SEPARATION

ALONG the Eastern shore the low waves creep,
   Making a ceaseless music on the sand,
   A song that gulls and curlews understand,
The lullaby that sings the day to sleep.
A thousand miles afar, the grim pines keep
   Unending watch upon a shoreless land,
   Yet through their tops, swept by some wizard hand,
The sound of surf comes singing up the steep.

Sweet, thou canst hear the tidal litany ;
   I, mid the pines land-wearied, may but dream
   Of the far shore ; but though the distance seem
Between us fixed, impassable, to me
   Cometh thy soul's voice, chanting love's old theme,
And mine doth answer, as the pines the sea.

ABSENT

My friend, I need thee in good days or ill,
  I need the counsel of thy larger thought;
  And I would question all the year has brought —
What spoil of books, what victories of will;
But most I long for the old wordless thrill,
  When on the shore, like children picture-taught,
  We watched each miracle the sweet day wrought,
While the tide ebbed, and every wind was still.

Dear, let it be again as if we mused,
  We two, with never need of spoken word
    (While the sea's fingers twined among the dulse,
And gulls dipped near), our spirits seeming fused
  In the great Life that quickens wave and bird,
    Our hearts in happy rhythm with the world-pulse.

THUS FAR

BECAUSE my life has lain so close to thine,
　　Because our hearts have kept a common beat,
　　Because thine eyes turned towards me frank and
　　　　sweet,
Reveal sometimes thine untold thoughts to mine,
Think not that I, by curious design,
　　Or over-step of too impetuous feet,
　　Could desecrate thy soul's supreme retreat,
Could disregard its quivering barrier-line.

Only a simple Levite, I, who stand
　　On the world's side of the most holy place,
　　Till, as the new day glorifies the east,
One come to lift the veil with reverent hand,
　　And enter with thy soul's soul face to face, —
　　He whom thy God shall call to be high priest.

THOUGHTS

THE morning brought a stranger to my door.
  I know not whence such feet as his may stray,
  From what still heights, along what star-set way.
  A child he seemed, yet my eyes fell before
His eyes Olympian.   I did implore
  Him enter, linger but one golden day
  To bless my house.   He passed, he might not stay,
  And though I call with tears, he comes no more.

At noon there stole a beggar to my gate,
  Of subtle tongue, the porter he beguiled.
  His creeping, evil steps my house defiled.
I flung him scornful alms, I bade him straight
  To leave me.   Swift he clutched my fee and smiled,
  Yet went not forth, nor goes, despite my hate.

CHRISTMAS

THE Christmas bells ring discord overhead;
  The Christmas lights flash cold across the snow;
  The angel-song fell silent long ago;
  Nor seer, nor silly shepherd comes, star-led,
To kneel to-night beside a baby's bed.
  Peace is not yet, and wrong and want and woe
  Cry in the city streets, and love is slow,
  And sin is sleek and swift and housed and fed.

Dear Lord, our faith is faint, our hearts are sore;
  Our prayers are as complaints, our songs as cries;
  Fain would we hear the angel-voice once more,
And see the Star still lead along the skies;
  Fain would, like sage and simple folk of yore,
  Watch where the Christ-child smiles in Mary's eyes.

SIDNEY LANIER

DIED SEPTEMBER 7, 1881

THE Southwind brought a voice; was it of bird?
  Or faint-blown reed? or string that quivered long?
  A haunting voice that woke into a song
Sweet as a child's low laugh, or lover's word.
We listened idly till it grew and stirred
  With throbbing chords of joy, of love, of wrong;
  A mighty music, resonant and strong;
Our hearts beat higher for that voice far-heard.

The Southwind brought a shadow, purple-dim,
  It swept across the warm smile of the sun;
    A sudden shiver passed on field and wave;
The grasses grieved along the river's brim.
  We knew the voice was silent, the song done;
    We knew the shadow smote across a grave.

RONDEAUS

"IF SPIRITS WALK"

"I have heard (but not believed) the spirits of the dead
May walk again."
                                        Winter's Tale.

IF spirits walk, Love, when the night climbs slow
The slant footpath where we were wont to go,
  Be sure that I shall take the self-same way
  To the hill-crest, and shoreward, down the gray,
Sheer, gravelled slope, where vetches straggling grow.

Look for me not when gusts of winter blow,
When at thy pane beat hands of sleet and snow;
  I would not come thy dear eyes to affray,
            If spirits walk.

But when, in June, the pines are whispering low,
And when their breath plays with thy bright hair so
  As some one's fingers once were used to play —
  That hour when birds leave song, and children
            pray,
Keep the old tryst, sweetheart, and thou shalt know
            If spirits walk.

19

I SAW LOVE'S EYES

I SAW Love's eyes, I saw Love's crownèd hair;
I heard Love's voice, a song across the air;
    The glad-of-heart were of Love's royal train;
    Sweet-throated heralds cried his endless reign,
And where his garment swept, the earth grew fair.

Along Love's road one walked whose feet were bare
And bleeding; no complaint he made, nor prayer,
    Yet dim and wistful as a child's in pain
              I saw Love's eyes.

I groped with Love where shadow lay, and snare;
I climbed with Love the icy mountain stair;
    The wood was dark, the height was hard to gain;
    The birds were songless and the flowers were
        slain;
Yet brave alway above my heart's despair
              I saw Love's eyes.

ACROSS THE FIELDS

Across the fields, the happy fields that lay
Unfaded yet, one visionary day
   We walked together, and the world was sweet.
   Each heard the whisper neither might repeat,
Love's whisper underneath our light word-play.

When fields were brown, when skies hung close
      and gray,
Alone I walked the dear familiar way,
   With eager heart, with hurrying love-led feet,
       Across the fields.

O life that hath so bitter words to say!
O heart so sore impatient of delay!
   O wistful hands that reach and may not meet!
   O eyes that yearn for answering eyes to greet!
The summer comes. It wins me not to stray
       Across the fields.

I SPEAK YOUR NAME

I SPEAK your name in alien ways, while yet
November smiles from under lashes wet.
   In the November light I see you stand
   Who love the fading woods and withered land,
Where Peace may walk, and Death, but not Regret.

The year is slow to alter or forget;
June's glow and autumn's tenderness are met.
   Across the months by this swift sunlight spanned,
        I speak your name.

Because I loved your golden hair, God set
His sea between our eyes. I may not fret,
   For, sure and strong, to meet my soul's demand,
   Comes your soul's truth, more near than hand in
      hand;
And low to God, who listens, Margaret,
        I speak your name.

MIGNONNE

FOURTEENTH CENTURY FORM

MIGNONNE, whose face bends low for my caressing,
  New and unknown to-night thy beauty seemeth;
  Dimly I read thine eyes as one who dreameth.

The moonlight yester-eve fell soft in blessing,
  That coldly now across thy bright hair gleameth;
Mignonne, whose face bends low for my caressing,
  New and unknown to-night thy beauty seemeth.

As penitent, low-voiced, his sins confessing,
  Pleads where the light of the high altar streameth,
  I speak to thee, whose love my love redeemeth.
Mignonne, whose face bends low for my caressing,
  New and unknown to-night thy beauty seemeth;
  Dimly I read thine eyes as one who dreameth.

SONGS

ARMISTICE

THE water sings along our keel,
  The wind falls to a whispering breath;
I look into your eyes and feel
  No fear of life or death;
So near is love, so far away
The losing strife of yesterday.

We watch the swallow skim and dip;
  Some magic bids the world be still;
Life stands with finger upon lip;
  Love hath his gentle will;
Though hearts have bled, and tears have burned,
The river floweth unconcerned.

We pray the fickle flag of truce
  Still float deceitfully and fair;
Our eyes must love its sweet abuse;
  This hour we will not care,
Though just beyond to-morrow's gate,
Arrayed and strong, the battle wait.

EVEN-SONG

Come, O Love, while the far stars whiten,
  Gathering, growing, momently;
Thou, who art star of stars, to lighten
  One dim heart that waiteth thee.

Speak, O Love, for the silence presses,
  Bowing my spirit like a fear;
Thou, whose words are as caresses,
  Sweet, sole voice that I long to hear.

SONG

Thy face I have seen as one seeth
    A face in a dream,
Soft drifting before me as drifteth
    A leaf on the stream:
A face such as evermore fleeth
    From following feet,
A face such as hideth and shifteth
    Evasive and sweet.

Thy voice I have heard as one heareth
    Afar and apart,
The wood-thrush that rapturous poureth
    The song of his heart;
Who heedeth is blest, but who neareth
    In wary pursuit,
May see where the singer upsoareth,
    The forest is mute.

SONG

"O Love, thou art winged and swift,
  Yet stay with me evermore ! "
And I guarded my house with bolt and bar
  Lest Love fly forth at the door.

Without, in the world, 'twas cold,
  While Love and I together
Laughed and sang by my red hearth-fire,
  Nor knew it was winter weather.

Sweet Love would lull me to sleep,
  In his tireless arm caressed ;
His shadowing wings and burning eyes
  Like night and stars wrought rest.

And ever the beat of Love's heart
  As a chime rang at my ear ;
And ever Love's bending, beautiful face
  Covered me close from fear.

Was it long ere I waked alone?
A snow-drift whitened the floor;
I saw spent ashes upon my hearth
And Death in my open door.

SONG

I COME across the sea,
   (O ship, ride fast)!
True heart, I sail to thee;
   Sail home at last.
Yet ships there are that never reach their haven,
   Though glad they sail;
And hoarse laments of curlew and sea-raven
   Haunt every gale.

My ship lies at the pier
   (The tide's at turn);
No place she hath for fear
   From prow to stern.
O Love, the soul shall never miss its haven,
   Though it sail far,
Nor hoarse laments of curlew and sea-raven
   May reach yon star.

SONG

LAUGHTER that ringeth all day long
  In a world of dancing feet;
A heart attuned to a bird's wild song,
  As eager, as wayward and sweet.
Love, passing by, drew near and smiled:
"Ah, dear Love, wait, she is a child!"
Reluctantly he went his way:
"I shall come back another day."

A heavier-drooping lid, a line
  Gentler in curving cheek and chin;
Lips where joys tremble, where hopes shine;
  And something more — a storm within,
A heart that wakes to sudden fears,
And eyes that know the use of tears:
"Ah, cruel Love! to come and teach
A pain that knows nor name nor speech!"

Love stands aggrieved: "Farewell, I go!
  Take back thy child-heart's unconcern."

D   33

"Nay, nay! Thou shalt not leave me so!"
    She holds him fast with tears that burn.
"Sweet Love, I pray thee to abide.
If thou walk constant at my side,
Through doubt, through sorrow, through despair,
No pain can be too hard to bear."

SONG

Lady mine, so passing fair,
Would'st thou roses for thy hair?
Would'st thou lilies for thy hand?
Bid me pluck them where they stand.
Those are warm and red to see,
These are cold. Are both like thee?
Brow of lily, lip of rose,
Heart that no man living knows!
If one knelt beside thy feet,
Would'st thou spurn, or love him, Sweet?

Hast seen the blue wave sleeping, sleeping,
  By gentle winds caressed?
Hast seen the far moon ceaseless keeping
  Her watch above its rest?

Hast seen the pale moths drift together
  With wingèd seeds wind-sown?
Hast seen the falling of gull's feather,
  Or leaf from wild rose blown?

Hast seen the white wave dancing, dancing,
  With wondrous witchery,
Like hers who rose, men's hearts entrancing,
  From out the sun-bright sea?

Lighter than wave, or leaf, or pinion,
  Than circling moth more fleet,
Than goddess mightier of dominion,
  The charm of rhythmic feet.

II

O day thou art so weary long !
  O night so maddening brief !
Swift moments for life's feast and song,
  Slow hours for life's grief.

A thousand pearls the lavish sea
  Rolls up to fill my hands ;
The ebb-tide leaves but shells to me
  Empty upon the sands.

BUD AND ROSE

FOR A CHILD

It is so small !
A cup of green, — a tiny tip
As pink as is a baby's lip,
    And that is all.

But sunshine's kiss,
And rain-drops falling warm and fast,
And coaxing winds will make at last
    A rose like this.

A WINTER SONG

ALL the roses are under the snow:
    Only the tips
Of the bare, brown, thorny bushes show.
    Out of sight, pretty blossoms sleep
Sweet and sound; there are left for me
Fairest of roses, one, two, three, —
    Where do you think?
On my baby's cheeks two, pale and pink,
    And one that is ripe and red and deep,
    On my baby's lips.

All the bonnie brown birds are flown
    Far to the South.
Never a piping, fluted tone,
    Never a silver, soaring song
From wood-path sounds, or meadow white;
Yet, in his hurried southward flight,
    Some songster kind
Has left the sweetest of gifts behind:

Music that ripples all day long
From my baby's mouth.

All the stars have faded away;
The blue bright skies
Show not a golden gleam to-day
Where a thousand flashed last night;
But when the far lamps blaze again,
For the brightest you may look in vain
(Sly truants two),
Fast hidden away from me and you,
Under soft covers folded tight
In my baby's eyes.

OTHER LYRICS

PRONE on the northern water,
  That laps him about the breast,
Like the Sphinx in the sand, forever
  The giant lies in rest.

The sails drive swift before him,
  And the surf beats at his lip,
But the gray eyes look out seaward
  Noting nor wave nor ship.

The centuries drift over,
  He marks not with smile nor frown,
Drift over him cloud and sea-gull,
  Swallow and thistledown.

I, of the race that passes,
  Quick with its hope and its fear,
Lean on his brow and question,
  Plead at his senseless ear:

"What of thy past unmeasured?
    And what of the peoples gone?
What of the sea's first singing?
    What of the primal dawn?

"What was the weird that bowed thee?
    How did the struggle cease?
Out of what Titan anguish
    Issued thy hopeless peace?"

Nothing the pale lips utter,
    What hath been, nor what shall be;
Under the brow's stern shadow,
    The gray eyes look to sea.

The blue glows round and over,
    Thin-veiled, as it were God's face;
I feel the breath, the spirit,
    That knows nor time nor space.

And my heart grieves for the giant
    In his pitiful repose,
Mocked by the vagrant gladness
    Of a laggard brier-rose;

Mocked to his face from seaward
  By the flash and whirl of wings;
Mocked from the grass above him,
  By life that creeps and sings.

I care not for his wisdom,
  His secret unconfessed;
I yearn toward rose and cricket,
  Ephemeral and blest.

Ah! if he might, how would he
  Quicken to love and to tears;
For my immortal minute
  Barter his endless years!

He rests on the restless water,
  And I on the grasses brown,
Drift over us cloud and sea-gull,
  Swallow and thistledown.

CASCO BAY.

VESPERS

The robins call me sweet and shrill:
   "Come out and fare afield;
The sun has neared the western hill,
The shadows slip down sure and still,
  But in our meadow wide and wet
  There's half an hour of sunshine yet;
    Come down, come down!" Who would not
    yield?

Across the road and through the lane,
   Where buttercups grow tall and bright
With daisies washed in last night's rain, —
Beyond the open bars I gain
  An angle of the rude rail-fence,
  A perfect coign of vantage, whence
    Wheat-field and pasture stretch in sight.

The cows, with stumbling tread and slow,
   One after one come straggling by,

And many a yellow head falls low,
And many a daisy's scattered snow,
  Where the unheeding footsteps pass,
  Is crushed and blackened in the grass,
    With brier and rue that trampled lie.

Sweet sounds with sweeter blend and strive :
    In its white prime of blossoming
Each wayside berry-bush, alive
With myriad bees, hums like a hive ;
  The frogs are loud in ditch and pool,
  And songs unlearned of court or school
    June's troubadours all round me sing.

Somewhere beneath the meadow's veil
    The peewee's brooding notes begin ;
The sparrows chirp from rail to rail ;
Above the bickering swallows sail,
  Or skim the green half-tasselled wheat
  With plaintive cry ; and at my feet
    A cricket tunes his mandolin.

High-perched, a master-minstrel proud,
    The red-winged blackbird pipes and calls,
One moment jubilant and loud,

The next, to sudden silence vowed,
Seeks cover in the marsh below ;
Soft winds along the rushes blow,
And like a whisper twilight falls.

GABRIEL

"That annunciation naméd death."

"I KNOW thee Angel, though thou dost not wear,
　As thou wast wont, the glory and the gold
　That smote upon the poet's gaze of old.
Thou Messenger! What tidings dost thou bear?

"I know thee winged and vested thus in gray,
　Not clouds of heaven and night of earth disguise
　The light supernal of thine awful eyes.
O Angel, linger, speak to me who pray!"

Almost I seemed to hold and to let slip
　The angel's robe; I know the gray wings cast
　Shadow about me; yet he smiled and passed,
That word of God a-quiver on his lip.

When morning came, one died whom I held dear;
　The angel's smile lay on his quiet face;
　For him who pleaded not had been the grace,
The word ineffable I wait to hear.

THOUGH UNSEEN

FROM the dwelling-place of the Holy Dead
  Wilt thou come back to me?
      O Love, it is far
      To that glad, great star
Whose shining hath hidden thee!
"Neither in star nor sun," she said,
  Her voice as it oft had been,
"The dwelling-place of the Holy Dead,
  Nor dreamer nor saint hath seen."

Lost Love of mine, where we walked of yore
  Thy feet made hallowed ground;
      Now earth is earth,
      Here are death and birth,
But where is the glory found?
Low at my side her voice once more,
  "Dull are thine eyes," she said;
"Walk with me now as we went of yore,"
  And I walk with the Holy Dead.

SANGRAAL

TASTING the wine of death he found it sweet;
Drank deeper draughts and only smiled the more;
As if he touched the hand that held the cup,
As if he saw the Christ look down on him,
Content he whispered, " Lord, I drink to thee."

WHEN NATURE HATH BETRAYED THE HEART THAT LOVED HER

THE gray waves rock against the gray sky-line,
  And break complaining on the long gray sand,
  Here where I sit who cannot understand
Their voice of pain nor this dumb pain of mine;

For I, who thought to fare till my days end,
  Armed sorrow-proof in sorrow, having known
  How hearts bleed slow when brave lips make no
    moan,
How Life can torture, how Death may befriend

When Love entreats him hasten,—even I,
  Who feared no human anguish that may be,
  I cannot bear the loud grief of the sea;
I cannot bear the still grief of the sky.

IN APRIL

ALL day the grass made my feet glad;
  I watched the bright life thrill
To each leaf-tip and flower-lip;
  Swift winds that swept the hill,
In garden nook light lingering, shook
  The budding daffodil.

I know not if the earth have kept
  Work-day or festival:
The sparrow sings of nestling things,
  Blithely the robins call;
And loud I hear, from marsh-pools near,
  The hylas at nightfall.

A LAND-WIND

The lichen rustles against my cheek,
  But the heart of the rock is still;
With chattering voice the cedars speak,
  Crouched gray on the barren hill.

A land-wind snarls on the cliff's sheer edge,
  Below, the smitten sea
Comes fawning over a sunken ledge,
  And cowers whimperingly.

In the sultry wood lies a restless hush,
  Not a twitter falls from the sky;
Hidden are swallow, sparrow and thrush,
  And the sea-birds only cry.

AT SEA

So many eves the sun must sink within
The westward plain of shoreless, homeless sea;
So many morns, as if from heaven to heaven,
From out the widening water in the east
The sun must rise; so many summer days,
Full in the face of the unveilèd sky,
The ship must float, till even the strongest gull,
Deserting, wheels to track a land-bound sail.
So many days! Yet there shall come a day —
Some golden, holy, August afternoon —
When, tired of sea at eve and sea at morn,
The sun shall droop like a contented child,
And sleep among the cradling hills of home.

FEBRUARY

Last night I heard a robin sing;
  And though I walked where woods were bare,
  And winds were cold, life quivered there,
As if in sleep the heart of spring
Were moved to dim remembering.
  To-day no promise haunts the air;
  I find but snow and silence where
Last night I heard a robin sing.

GHOSTS

I SLEPT last night and dreamed,
I woke and cried,
For in my sleep it seemed
Close by my side,
Walked still and slow the old days that have died.

All ghostly slow they passed,
All ghostly still ;
Of old who fled so fast,
With life a-thrill,
With laughing lips and eyes, with eager will.

So ghostlike, yet the same,
Each dear dead day,
Softly I called her name
And bade her stay ;
Softly she turned and smiled and went her way.

SLEEP

DEAR gray-eyed Angel, wilt thou come to-night?
  Spread the soft shadow of thy sheltering wings,
And banish every hint of thought and light,
  And all the clamoring crowd of waking things?
Wilt thou bend low above wide weary eyes,
As o'er the worn world bend the tireless skies?

THE WATCHER AND THE WIND

THE WATCHER

WILD singer at my casement, be thou still!
  In pity let me sleep;
For I am weary, and thy voice is shrill;
  We have no tryst to keep.
Go on thy way; to gladder hearts than mine
  Thy song perchance were glad;
To me if thou must come, come with sunshine,
  For night is over sad.

THE WIND

Nay listen, listen thou so fretfully pleading for rest;
  Those whom I rock may sleep:
I rock drowned men in ocean cradled deep,
  And birds in frozen nest.

THE MADONNA

THE years may enter not her shrine;
  Forever fair and young she stands,
  And with her gracious, girlish hands
Folds tenderly the child divine.

Her lips are warm with mother-love
  And blessedness, and from her eyes
  Looks the mute, questioning surprise
Of one who hears a voice above

Life's voices, — from the throng apart,
  Listens to God's low-whispered word
  (Strange message by no other heard),
And keeps his secret in her heart.

Sweet maiden-mother, years have fled
  Since the great painter dropped his brush,
  Left earth's loud praise for heaven's kind hush,
While men bewailed him, early dead, —

Yet mothers kneel before thee still
  Uplifting happy hearts ; or, wild
  With cruel loss, reach toward thy child
Void arms for the Christ-love to fill.

Time waits without the sacred spot
  Where fair and young the mother stands ;
  Time waits, and bars with jealous hands
The door where years may enter not.

PAN AND PSYCHE

(A PAINTING BY SIR EDWARD BURNE-JONES)

SWEET Psyche, hath thy quest of Love
So led thee to a sterile land,
Only to grief and fear at last?
What stranger this who bends above
Thy beauty? What unshapely hand
Hides in the glory of thy hair?
Pale wanderer, thy long sorrows past,
May find no solace in those eyes,
Though wistfully they scrutinize
Thy face, and, dimly, know it fair.

Go thou thy way bright Love to find;
And in the bliss of his embrace
Thou shalt forget Pan's dusky face.
Go thou thy way bright Love to find;
While Pan, forsaken, like a brute

Turns to his fare of nut and root;
Yet change hath passed on the dark mind:
Nor god nor beast now, from his flute
Low human music haunts the wind.

A SMILING DEMON OF NÔTRE DAME

Quiet as are the quiet skies
He watches where the city lies
Floating in vision clear or dim
Through sun or rain beneath his eyes;
Her songs, her laughter and her cries
Hour after hour drift up to him.

Her days of glory or disgrace
He watches with unchanging face;
He knows what midnight crimes are done;
What horrors under summer sun;
And souls that pass in holy death
Sweep by him on the morning's breath.

Alike to holiness and sin
He feels nor alien nor akin;

Five hundred creeping mortal years
He smiles on human joy and tears,
Man-made, immortal, scorning man ;
Serene, grotesque Olympian.

F

THE COMMON CHORD

A POET sang, so light of heart was he,
  A song that thrilled with joy in every word;
It quivered with ecstatic melody;
It laughed as sunshine laughs upon the sea;
  It caught a measure from each lilting bird;
But though the song rang out exultantly,
    The world passed by, with heavy step and loud,
    None heeding, save that, parted from the crowd,
      Two lovers heard.

There fell a day when sudden sorrow smote
  The poet's life. Unheralded it came,
Blotting the sun-touched page whereon he wrote
His golden song. Ah! then, from all remote,
  He sang the grief that had nor hope nor name
In God's ear only; but one sobbing note
    Reached the world's heart, and swiftly, in the wake
    Of bitterness and passion and heart-break,
      There followed fame.

DESTINY

A NOISOME thing that crawls by covert path,
  For glad, unfearing feet to lie in wait;
No part in summer's fellowship it hath,
  From mirth and love and music alienate.

Yet once it flashed across the close, brown grass
  In the noon sun, and, as it quivered there,
The spell of beauty over it did pass,
  Making it kin with earth and light and air.

I knew that Life's imperial self decrees
  That this, the loathliest of living things,
By patient ways of cycled centuries,
  Slow creeping, shall at last attain to wings.

RIVER AND BIRD

FLOWETH the river still and strong;
Flitteth the bird swift-winged along
Its crested wave with joyous song.

The bird is a creature of air and light;
Skyward she taketh her circling flight,
Leaving the broad stream out of sight.

What though the mighty river frets
With broken voice? Of long regrets
Light hearts know little. The bird forgets.

Weary at last of all things fair;
Weary of soaring everywhere;
Weary of heaven, and earth, and air;

Discontent in the song she sings —
Cometh the bird from her wanderings
Back to the river to dip her wings.

*   *   *   *   *

Stealeth the noon-hush far and wide ;
Smileth the sun on the river's tide ;
Dreameth the bird in the shade beside.

*   *   *   *   *

My love is the river still and strong ;
Thy heart is the bird that flits along
Wave and ripple, with joyous song.

A JOURNEY

Uprose the Day when Night lay dead,
  She turned not back to kiss his cheek,
  But o'er the sombre eastern peak
She soared, and touched it into red.

Her strong wings scattered mist and cloud,
  As swiftly toward the highest blue,
  Unhindered, radiant, she flew.
She sang for joy; she laughed aloud.

"The midmost heaven," she cried, "is mine!
  The midmost heaven and half the earth.
  A million joys I bring to birth,
Upon a million lovers shine!

"I paint the grape, I gild the corn,
  I float the lilies on the lake,
  I set athrill in field and brake
Fine strains of tiny flute and horn.

"Ah, it is sweet," she said, and passed,
  Exulting still, down the sheer slope
  Of afternoon. Her heart of hope
Went with her, dauntless, till, at last,

Upon the far low-lying range
  Of hills, she spread a crimson cloud;
  From the pale mists she tore a shroud,
And, sinking, faint with sense of change,

She seemed to see a face bend o'er
  With kind, familiar eyes. She said:
  "Can it be you I left for dead?
Can it be Night?" and spoke no more.

Night wrapped her in his mantle gray;
  He kissed the quivering lids that slept;
  He bowed his silver head and wept —
"How could she know, my love, my Day?"

A DREAM

Last night, what time dreams wander east and west,
  What time a dream may linger, I lay dead,
  With flare of tapers pale above my head,
With weight of drifted roses on my breast;
And they, who noiseless came to watch my rest,
  Looked kindly down and gentle sentence said.

One sighed "She was but young to go to-day;"
  And one "How fiercely life with death had striven
  Ere God set free her spirit, sorrow-shriven!"
One said "The children grieve for her at play;"
And one, who bent to take a rose away,
  Whispered "Dear love, would that we had for-
      given."

SIDNEY LANIER

"Let my name perish: the poetry is good poetry, and the music is good music; and beauty dieth not, and the heart that needs it will find it." — Sidney Lanier (letter to his wife).

BEFORE his eyes forever shone afar
The beauty that his strong soul loved and sought,
And fast he followed it nor looked behind;
No way too long, too rugged, nor too dark
For his intent, fixed will. Close after him
Sorrow and Pain sped on in swift pursuit;
He felt their hard hands clutch to hold him back;
Their breath was hot upon his fevered cheek;
His eyes were weary, and his feet dropped blood;
He fell at last, and yet, they were too late,
For folded close in his weak hand he held
The prize their strength was impotent to wrest.
Upon his forehead, growing white and chill,
His Love, his Art laid gentle hands that blessed,
And on his spirit fell his Master's peace.

ENTRE NOUS

I TALK with you of foolish things and wise,
  Of persons, places, books, desires, and aims,
Yet all our words a silence underlies,
  An earnest, vivid thought that neither names.

Ah! what to us were foolish talk or wise?
  Were persons, places, books, desires, or aims
Without the deeper sense that underlies,
  The sweet encircling thought that neither names?

COMMUNION

Dusk of a lowering evening,
  Chill of a northern zone,
Pitiful press of worn faces,
  And an exiled heart alone.

Warm, as with sun of the tropic,
  Keen, as with salt of the sea,
Sweet, as with breath of blown roses,
  Cometh thy thought to me.

THE RIDER

One rode slow by river and wood :
  Slow and still, on the wayside grass ;
And the willows withered where they stood,
  As they felt the silent rider pass.

He drew rein nor at hut nor hall ;
  Only smiled and rode his way ;
Yet a strong man turned him to the wall ;
  And a child waked not with the waking day.

The rider spurred to the city gate ;
  None gave him welcome where he came ;
Glad eyes grew hard, for fear and hate,
  And pale lips quivered with his name.

Slow, again, by river and wood
  The horseman went on the blackened grass ;
The leafless willows shivering stood,
  As they felt the silent rider pass.

A GREETING

My day was sordid and perplexed,
  Close circled by the commonplace ;
And late I walked with spirit vexed,
  And sense of self-disgrace ;
For life and I were out of tune ;
  I did not see the rose-like flush ;
  I did not feel the kindly hush
Of waning afternoon.

Its glory all around me lay,
  While yet I paced in discontent ;
When, suddenly, from far away,
  A quivering flash was sent ;
It thrilled my heart, it stayed my feet,
  A beacon sure and glad it shone,
  The last red gleam of day upon
Your westward window, Sweet.

And straight I knew the world was fair ;
  I heard a robin's prophet song ;

I drank the bright wine of the air;
　My pulse grew quick and strong;
Not wasted seemed the day's work done;
　Not hopeless seemed the thing I sought;
　The far-off heights of toil and thought
Seemed worthy to be won.

FROM OVER-SEA

In Italy how comes the spring?
I look across wide fields of snow
To naked woods, and long to know
How fair the shimmering mountains lie?
How warm above them bends the sky
      Of Tuscany?
What word from Rome the swallows bring,
      Swift sent to thee?
Here stirs no life of bud nor wing;
The trees by icy winds are torn;
And yet I dream how flowers are born
      In Italy.

I see the far, fair city swim
Through mists of memory bright yet dim
Shining, even as it shone of old
Through Arno's haze of subtile gold,
      By witchery

Of distance, light and evening spun.
Tall cypresses against the sun
      Distinct I see,
Defiling darkly up the hill,
As when we wandered at our will
      In Italy.

TO ——

Madonna mia! if in truth
   Our Raphael from heaven's palaces
   Might lean across the centuries
That have not marred his glorious youth,

Nor dimmed the lustre of his hair,
   Nor dulled his pencil, rather grown
   Diviner, working near God's throne,
Even he might find a study fair

As his last fresco in the skies,
   Might pause untouched of mortal taint
   One infinite half hour to paint
The motherhood in your dear eyes.

APRIL

(FROM THE FRENCH OF REMY BELLEAU)

APRIL, thou art the smile
    That erewhile
Cypris wore ; and thy birth
Is so sweet that in heaven
    The gods even
Are breathing the perfume of earth.

'Tis thou, gracious and mild,
    Hast beguiled
Those exiles fleet of wing, —
Exiles long time afar,
    Swallows that are
The messengers faithful of spring.

METEMPSYCHOSIS

I WATCH thy face, Sweetheart, with half belief
  In olden tales of the soul's wayfaring;
  I marvel from what past thy young eyes bring
Their heritage of long entailèd grief.

I watch thy face and soft as through a dream
  I see not thee, but some fair, fated Greek,
  Whose carven lips grow flesh straightway and speak
Stern words and sad, with perfect curves that seem

But as the cynic sweetness of thy smile,
  Set quivering over tears in self-despite.
  Again I watch by mystic taper-light,
Where a pale saint doth kneel a weary while;

I hear the murmured passion of her prayer,
  Imploring heaven for boon of sacrifice;

I read behind the rapture of her eyes
A look which thou didst teach me unaware.

The visions pass; the light, but now so faint,
   Flames red and sudden over field and brook;
   Thy face is turned, full fronting me with look
Worn never yet of cynic nor of saint;

And now amid fierce Northern battle-glare,
   Where wounded heroes wait the gods' decree,
   The Valkyr rides, and o'er her brow I see
The floating golden glory of thy hair.

Sweet spirit, pilgrim through the cycled years,
   Dear though thou art I may not bid thee stay;
   I bless thee whatsoever chartless way
Thou goest, God-impelled.   I have no fears.

I know thou wilt surrender not to pain;
   Thou wilt look never forth from coward eyes;
   Thou would'st not barter truth for Paradise;
Thou could'st not think that ease and peace were
      gain.

Far off, I know, the darkness shall be light
  For him who scorneth to make terms with Fate ;
  Far off for thee, Belovèd, there must wait
The answered question, and the finished fight.

A LETTER

THE last light falls across your pictured face
(Unanswering sweet face, half turned away),
Withdrawing still, as down the west apace
Fades too the profile of June's longest day.
I wonder, did you watch an hour ago
While dropped the sun behind the mountain-line?
And did you think how it, retreating so,
Must blaze along this level world of mine?
Love, what have I to do with sunset skies,
How red soever? All the world for me
Spreads eastward, and before my spirit's eyes,
Set fair between the mountains and the sea,
Doth stand the distant city of my heart.

Forgive me if I tell myself in vain:
"There is no power in this wide world to part
Our souls. Avail not time nor space nor pain,

For love is unconditioned." Dear, to-night
I am like an unlessoned child, who cries
For the sweet sensual things of touch and sight;
I want to read the gladness in your eyes;
I want your voice though but to speak my name;
My heart uncomforted, unsatisfied,
Hath put my best philosophy to shame.

Yet if you crossed the shadows to my side,—
No vision, but your very self indeed,—
I should not ask what kindly fate had brought
My heart's desire. I should not find at need
Expression for one eager waiting thought,
Not one of all the words I have to say.
I should but lean my cheek upon your hand,
And hold you close, the old, mute, childish way,
And you would comfort me and understand.

But not to-night,—I will be patient, Sweet,
Sit silently, and let life have its will.
The tread of the last passer in the street
Sounds with the chiming hour, then all is still,
Save that the little fountain in the park
Sings lazily the same old summer song

You knew in quiet nights when winds lay furled.
I needs must dream alone here in the dark
A little while, to-morrow go forth strong,
Lifting the shield of Love against the world.

VENICE IN APRIL: A MEMORY

A GONDOLA motionless lying
Under the Arsenal wall;
A weary boatman at stern and at bow
Supinely stretched half asleep;
And you with eyes merrily deep
Silent to mine replying,
'Tis sweet to remember how.

We had floated far that day,
That happiest day of all!
The circling silver mountain-rim
Shut us safe from the world away;
Though eyes we loved were hurt and dim,
There came to us nor cry nor call,
Where, idle-oared, content we lay
Under the Arsenal wall.

On the ripple a quivering crescent
Tossed like a tortured thing,
But, far above, serene,

It hung in the curve of the sky;
At our prow was the gentle, incessant
Sound of the waves' caress,
Impelled by the light breath wandering by
From some ocean god unseen
In his palace of idleness;
And ever from two bell-towers
Rang out the quarter-hours,
In broken harmonies
Like the changes in a chaunt:
Sounds to stay in one's ears and haunt
One's dreams with perplexing memories.

Shoreward or seaward making,
The boats passed lazily;
We watched one golden sail that flew
(Its fellow-flock forsaking)
Before our eyes like a butterfly,
Afar where the sea-breeze fresher grew;
How it seemed to beckon from out the blue
Of the mystical, deepening southern sky,
Till we longed to follow, we two!

The fair day loitered to its close,
The boatmen awakened, the play-time was done;

The wide air turned to gold and rose,
And where we watched a passing rower,
We saw the water run
Drop by drop from his gleaming oar,
Opal and pearl and amethyst.

Eastward and westward grew the light;
San Marco's domes were floating mist;
The Campanile's slender height
Stood pale against one purple cloud,
Down which the sun dropped suddenly,
Piercing it through with a golden shaft.
We were silent now, none spoke nor laughed;
Only the bells anon rang loud,
Ever repeating to you and to me:
"The story is ended, the dream is o'er,
You may carry away beyond the sea
A picture, and nothing more."

And yet, might the dream of a dream avail,
'Twere good to dream it over again;
To forget the years that lie between,
To be careless of heart as then;
To see the glow of that warm rose light,

Feel the hush of that air serene;
Once more down the silvery, far lagune,
Under opal sky and crescent moon,
To follow that golden sail.

TO–DAY'S DAUGHTER

Written for the Graduating Class at Smith College, June, 1885

I

O VERY fair and strong she stands to-day,
  This youngest daughter to receive her dower;
I see the wise World-mother smiling lay
  Gift after gift before her, bid her choose
  The richest, purest, rarest, lest she lose
    One happiness, one power.

II

Thou wise World-mother! it was long to wait
    Hoarding thy treasures while the slow years
      passed,
Keeping thy cherished plan inviolate
  With thine inscrutable, sweet smile, until
  This golden hour has risen to fulfil
    Thy dearest wish at last

III

For this thy child, a woman earnest-eyed,
    Who wears thy gracious favours worthily,
Pledges her honest faith, her constant pride,
    To live her life as one who holds in trust
    God's gold to give again, who fearless must
        Face the great days to be.

IV

Naught is denied her : mind alert, intent ;
    Eyes that look deep into the heart of things ;
A skilful hand to shape ; a firm will bent
    On purposes that have no petty ends ;
    A strength that falters not for foes nor friends ;
        A soul that has swift wings.

V

Deep has she read of poet and of priest ;
    Wit of philosopher and lore of sage ;
And science, with its growth of great from least,
    Who bids earth's cowering, secret things appear,
    And stand out in this latter sunshine, clear
        As type upon God's page.

VI

Yet finds she wiser teachers, friends more dear,
  In shadowy wood-path and on clover slope;
When the June twilight slow and still creeps near,
  And rocks put on their purple majesty;
  When stars across the dark tell glimmeringly
    Her happy horoscope.

VII

And sometimes, when the low moon lies asleep
  On its cloud-bed, like a fair child, play-spent,
Across the river-fields and up the steep
  Come, silent stealing through the silver mist,
  Strange visitors, whose holy lips have kissed
    Death's own, yet are content.

VIII

Wide eyes that seem to bring from far-off years
  Their loves and hopes and tragedies again;
And voices sadly cadenced to young ears,
  Yet musical with old-time gentleness;
  And smiles that half conceal and half confess
    Some unforgotten pain.

IX

And one with voice that hath a dauntless ring,
    Saith, " From thy life, Sweet, may the gods avert
The need of this strange gift I dare to bring,
    A Roman woman's strength, who will not spare
    A quivering death-wound at the heart to wear,
        And say it doth not hurt."

X

Speaketh a voice whose sound is of the sea :
    " Oft have I paced the beach, while sheer above
Towered the rocks, waiting immutably
    As my heart waited. From Inarimé,
    Across the years, Vittoria brings to-day
        Her gift of tireless love."

XI

As starlight comes through myriad miles of space,
    Undimmed, untarnished, waxing never old,
So shineth (nor can centuries efface)
    One light set in the sky of time afar,
    Thy soul, Antigone, that like a star
        Burneth with flame of gold.

XII

Antigone, what woman were not glad
　　To feel against her life the touch of thine?
To meet thine eyes, so unafraid, if sad?
　　To hear thy words, to clasp thy potent hand?
　　To read thy womanhood as a command
　　To sacrifice divine?

XIII

Yet past nor present can avail to fill
　　This woman's thoughts, who leans and listens best
To voices of the future, calling shrill,
　　With strain and stress of troubled destinies,
　　Content she leaves her dreams and reveries
　　For life's sublime unrest.

XIV

With steadfast step she walks in darkened ways
　　Where women's curses sound, and children's
　　　　cries ;
Her gentleness shall win, her strength shall raise,
　　Her love shall cleanse, her righteous words shall
　　　　burn,

H

And wasted, piteous baby-lips shall learn
Glad laughter from her eyes.

XV

Shadow shall shrink, and sunlight shine for her;
  And love shall touch her life like a caress;
And loyal human hearts shall minister
  To her heart's need, who hath for joy, for pain,
  For sorrow's mourning, ay! and for sin's stain
  Unending tenderness.

XVI

Around her closes, quivering and tense,
  Life's narrow circle of perplexities;
The clamoring hours, the hurrying events;
  Yet shall she pass through tumult and through
    crowd
  Serene, as one who hears God's voice ring loud
  Across far silences.

* * * * * *

Who climbs life's mountain walks with tardy tread,
  For love of flowers that smile about his feet,
For love of pines that whisper overhead,

For love of wandering bird-calls, shy and sweet;
Yet where the birds come not, beyond the pines,
　Past rock and steep and cloud, the final height
　Forever rises silent, stainless white,
Where shadow never falls, where latest shines
　The lingering light.

THE POETICAL WORKS

OF

ALFRED AUSTIN,

POET LAUREATE.

LYRICAL POEMS. One vol. Crown 8vo. $1.75.

NARRATIVE POEMS. One vol. Crown 8vo. $1.75.

THE TOWER OF BABEL: A Celestial Love Drama. One vol. Crown 8vo. $1.75.

SAVONAROLA: A Tragedy. One vol. Crown 8vo. $1.75.

THE HUMAN TRAGEDY. One vol. Crown 8vo. $1.75.

PRINCE LUCIFER. One vol. Crown 8vo. $1.75.

FORTUNATUS THE PESSIMIST. One vol. Crown 8vo. $1.75.

MADONNA'S CHILD. One vol. Fcap 8vo. $1.00.

ENGLAND'S DARLING. With portrait. One vol. 12mo. $1.25.

MACMILLAN & CO.,
66 FIFTH AVENUE, NEW YORK.